Lily Wants to Fly

Written by Michèle Dufresne · Illustrated by Max Stasiuk

PIONEER VALLEY EDUCATIONAL PRESS, INC.

Here is Clarence.

Clarence is asleep.

Here is Lily.

Lily is not asleep.

"I like to fly," said Lily.

"I like to ride on Clarence."

"Wake up, Clarence," said Lily. "Wake up!"

"I am asleep," said Clarence.

"Come on, Clarence," said Lily. "Wake up. Can we go flying?"

"No!" said Clarence.

"I am asleep!"

"Come on, Clarence," said Lily. "Wake up. We can look for food to eat!"

"I like to eat," said Clarence.

"And I like to fly!" said Lily.